ARTHUR CHRISTMAS™

NO PRESENT LEFT BEHIND!

Adapted by
ANNIE AUERBACH

STERLING CHILDREN'S BOOKS
New York

An Imprint of Sterling Publishing
387 Park Avenue South
New York, NY 10016

ISBN 978-1-4027-9245-8 (trade paperback)

Distributed in Canada by Sterling Publishing
c/o Canadian Manda Group, 165 Dufferin Stree
Toronto, Ontario, Canada M6K 3H6
Distributed in the United Kingdom by GMC Distribution Services
Castle Place, 166 High Street, Lewes, East Sussex, England BN7 1XU
Distributed in Australia by Capricorn Link (Australia) Pty. Ltd.
P.O. Box 704, Windsor, NSW 2756, Australia

For information about custom editions, special sales, and premium and corporate purchases,
please contact Sterling Special Sales at 800-805-5489 or specialsales@sterlingpublishing.com.

Manufactured in Canada
Lot #:
2 4 6 8 10 9 7 5 3 1
09/11

www.sterlingpublishing.com/kids

It's Christmas Eve—the busiest night of the year. Santa has traded in his reindeer for the state-of-the-art S-1 sleigh. Luckily, he has a team of over a million highly-trained elves to help deliver all the presents. At the exact same time, they drop down to the rooftops. The Christmas clock is ticking down. They have only 18.14 seconds per house!

Santa's son, Steve, is in command of Santa's S-1 sleigh. He spends Christmas Eve stationed on the Mission Control deck. He monitors the weather, the elves on the ground, and any delivery drop problems. Steve knows which house has squeaky stairs and which one has a yappy dog. Steve has computerized Christmas with military precision.

Accidentally, a bicycle gets left behind. Arthur, Santa's younger son, believes in the magic of Christmas. Arthur and Grandsanta decide to deliver the present themselves. They pull out the original sleigh. They just need some reindeer and a little magic dust!

Arthur and Grandsanta take off from the North Pole. They fly up in the air. Grandsanta is having a jolly good time. Arthur is scared to death! Suddenly, Bryony, a Gift Wrapping Elf, pops out from her hiding spot. A stowaway!

Arthur is trying to deliver the bicycle to a little girl named Gwen who lives in England. But the trio ends up in Africa instead! It's not long before some very hungry lions find them. Luckily, Bryony and her sticky tape talents save the day!

The sun is rising. It's almost Christmas morning! Arthur has finally arrived at Gwen's house. Very quietly, he places her present under the tree. Arthur's mission is a complete success!

Gwen is excited to ride her new bike. She looks outside her front door. Is that Santa she sees?

Behind the Scenes

The amazing art and dynamic animation for *Arthur Christmas* was not made overnight. It took artists years to perfect every last detail of the characters and environments. Before making it to the big screen, the talented teams at Aardman Animations and Sony Pictures Animation created hundreds of character and location sketches, sculptures, and paintings for inspiration. Their CG (computer-generated) experts then took that hand-drawn artwork and used it as a basis for the final film you see in theaters. Here is some "behind-the-scenes" art that shows how *Arthur Christmas* came to life!

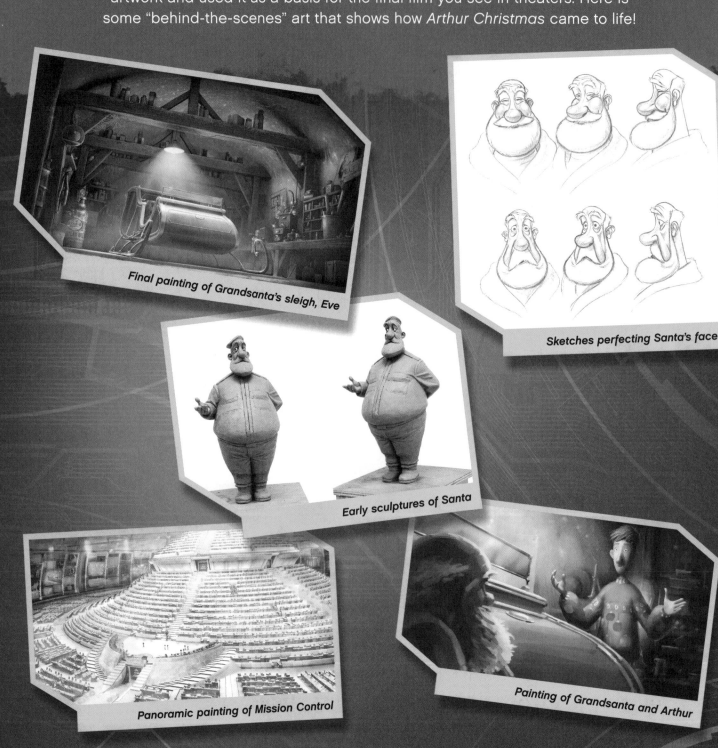

Final painting of Grandsanta's sleigh, Eve

Sketches perfecting Santa's face

Early sculptures of Santa

Panoramic painting of Mission Control

Painting of Grandsanta and Arthur